ST. JOHN'S EVE

ST. JOHN'S EVE

NIKOLAI GOGOL

WILDSIDE PRESS

Published by Wildside Press LLC.
www.wildsidebooks.com

Thoma Grigroovitch had one very strange eccentricity: to the day of his death he never liked to tell the same thing twice. There were times when, if you asked him to relate a thing afresh, he would interpolate new matter, or alter it so that it was impossible to recognise it. Once upon a time, one of those gentlemen who, like the usurers at our yearly fairs, clutch and beg and steal every sort of frippery, and issue mean little volumes, no thicker than an A B C book, every month, or even every week, wormed this same story out of Thoma Grigorovitch, and the latter completely forgot about it. But that same young gentleman, in the pea-green caftan, came from Poltava, bringing with him a little book, and, opening it in the middle, showed it to us. Thoma Grigorovitch was on the point of setting his spectacles astride of his nose, but recollected that he had forgotten to wind thread about them and stick them together with wax, so he passed it over to me. As I understand nothing about reading and writing, and do not wear spectacles, I undertook to read it. I had not turned two leaves when all at once he caught me by the hand and stopped me.

"Stop! tell me first what you are reading."

I confess that I was a trifle stunned by such a question.

"What! what am I reading, Thoma Grigorovitch? Why, your own words."

"Who told you that they were my words?"

"Why, what more would you have? Here it is printed: 'Related by such and such a sacristan.'"

"Spit on the head of the man who printed that! he lies, the dog of a Moscow pedlar! Did I say that? ''Twas just the same as though one hadn't his wits about him!' Listen. I'll tell the tale to you on the spot."

We moved up to the table, and he began.

* * * *

My grandfather (the kingdom of heaven be his! may he eat only wheaten rolls and poppy-seed cakes with honey in the other world!) could tell a story wonderfully well. When he used to begin a tale you could not stir from the spot all day, but kept on listening. He was not like the story-teller of the present day, when he begins to lie, with a tongue as though he had had nothing to eat for three days, so that you snatch your cap and flee from the house. I remember my old mother was alive then, and in the long winter evenings when the frost was crackling out of doors, and had sealed up hermetically the narrow panes of our cottage, she used to sit at her wheel, drawing out a long thread in her hand, rocking the cradle with her foot, and humming a song, which I seem to hear even now.

The lamp, quivering and flaring up as though in fear of something, lighted up our cottage; the spindle hummed; and all of us children, collected in a cluster, listened to grandfather, who had not crawled off the stove for more than five years, owing to his great age. But the wondrous tales of the incursions of the Zaporozhian Cossacks and the Poles, the bold deeds of Podkova, of Poltar-Kozhukh, and Sagaidatchnii, did not interest us so much as the stories about some deed of old which always sent a shiver through our frames and made our hair rise upright on our heads. Sometimes such terror took possession of us in consequence of them, that, from that evening forward, Heaven knows how wonderful everything seemed to us. If one chanced to go out of the cottage after nightfall for anything, one fancied that a visitor from the other world had lain down to sleep in one's bed; and I have often taken my own smock, at a distance, as it lay at the head of the bed, for the Evil One rolled up into a ball! But the chief thing about grandfather's stories was, that he never lied in all his life; and whatever he said was so, was so.

I will now tell you one of his wonderful tales. I know that there are a great many wise people who copy in the courts, and can even read civil documents, but who, if you were to put into their hand a simple prayer-book, could not make out the first letter in it, and would show all their teeth in derision. These people laugh at everything you tell them. Along comes one of them — and doesn't believe in witches! Yes, glory to God that I have lived so long in the world! I have seen heretics to whom it would be easier to lie in confession than it would be to our brothers and equals to take snuff, and these folk would deny the existence of witches! But let them just dream about something, and they won't even tell what it was! There, it is no use talking about them!

No one could have recognised the village of ours a little over a hundred years ago; it was a hamlet, the poorest kind of a hamlet. Half a score of miserable farmhouses, unplastered and badly thatched, were scattered here and there about the fields. There was not a yard or a decent shed to shelter animals or waggons. That was the way the wealthy lived: and if you had looked for our brothers, the poor — why, a hole in the ground — that was a cabin for you! Only by the smoke could you tell that a God-created man lived there. You ask why they lived so? It was not entirely through poverty: almost every one led a raiding Cossack life, and gathered not a little plunder in foreign lands; it was rather because it was little use building up a good wooden house. Many folk were engaged in raids all over the country — Crimeans, Poles, Lithuanians!

It was quite possible that their own countrymen might make a descent and plunder everything. Anything was possible.

In this hamlet a man, or rather a devil in human form, often made his appearance. Why he came, and whence, no one knew. He prowled about, got drunk, and suddenly disappeared as if into the air, leaving no trace of his existence. Then, behold, he seemed to have dropped from the sky again, and went flying about the street of the village, of which no trace now remains, and which was not more than a hundred paces from Dikanka. He would collect together all the Cossacks he met; then there were songs, laughter, and cash in plenty, and vodka flowed like water. . . . He would address the pretty girls, and give them ribbons, earrings, strings of beads — more than they knew what to do with. It is true that the pretty girls rather hesitated about accepting his presents: God knows, perhaps, what unclean hands they had passed through. My grandfather's aunt, who kept at that time a tavern, in which Basavriuk (as they called this devil-man) often caroused, said that no consideration on the earth would have induced her to accept a gift from him. But then, again, how avoid accepting? Fear seized on every one when he knit his shaggy brows, and gave a sidelong glance which might send your feet God knows whither: whilst if you did accept, then the next night some fiend from the swamp, with horns on his head, came and began to squeeze your neck, if there was a string of beads upon it; or bite your finger, if there was a ring upon it; or drag you by the hair, if ribbons were braided in it. God have mercy, then, on those who held such gifts! But here was the difficulty: it was impossible to get rid of them; if you threw them into the water, the diabolical ring or necklace would skim along the surface and into your hand.

There was a church in the village — St. Pantelei, if I remember rightly. There lived there a priest, Father Athanasii of blessed memory. Observing that Basavriuk did not come to church, even at Easter, he determined to reprove him and impose penance upon him. Well, he hardly escaped with his life. "Hark ye, sir!" he thundered in reply, "learn to mind your own business instead of meddling in other people's, if you don't want that throat of yours stuck with boiling kutya[1]." What was to be done with this unrepentant man? Father Athanasii contented himself with announcing that any one who should make the acquaintance of Basavriuk would be counted a Catholic, an enemy of Christ's orthodox church, not a member of the human race.

In this village there was a Cossack named Korzh, who had a labourer whom people called Peter the Orphan — perhaps because no one remembered either his father or mother. The church elder, it is true, said that they had died of the pest in his second year; but my grandfather's aunt would not hear of that, and tried with all her might to furnish him with parents, although poor Peter needed them about as much as we need last year's snow. She said that his father had been in Zaporozhe, and had been taken prisoner by the Turks, amongst whom he underwent God only knows what tortures, until having, by some miracle, disguised himself as a eunuch, he made his escape. Little cared the black-browed youths and maidens about Peter's parents. They merely remarked, that if he only had a new coat, a red sash, a black lambskin cap with a smart blue crown on his head, a Turkish sabre by his side, a whip in one hand and a pipe with handsome mountings in the other, he would surpass all the young men. But the pity was, that the only thing poor Peter had was a grey gaberdine with more holes in it than there are gold pieces in a Jew's pocket. But that was not the worst of it. Korzh had a daughter, such a beauty as I think you can hardly have chanced to see.

---

1   A dish of rice or wheat flour, with honey and raisins, which is brought to the church on the celebration of memorial masses.

My grandfather's aunt used to say — and you know that it is easier for a woman to kiss the Evil One than to call any one else a beauty — that this Cossack maiden's cheeks were as plump and fresh as the pinkest poppy when, bathed in God's dew, it unfolds its petals, and coquets with the rising sun; that her brows were evenly arched over her bright eyes like black cords, such as our maidens buy nowadays, for their crosses and ducats, off the Moscow pedlars who visit the villages with their baskets; that her little mouth, at sight of which the youths smacked their lips, seemed made to warble the songs of nightingales; that her hair, black as the raven's wing, and soft as young flax, fell in curls over her shoulders, for our maidens did not then plait their hair in pigtails interwoven with pretty, bright-hued ribbons. Eh! may I never intone another alleluia in the choir, if I would not have kissed her, in spite of the grey which is making its way through the old wool which covers my pate, and of the old woman beside me, like a thorn in my side! Well, you know what happens when young men and maidens live side by side. In the twilight the heels of red boots were always visible in the place where Pidorka chatted with her Peter. But Korzh would never have suspected anything out of the way, only one day — it is evident that none but the Evil One could have inspired him — Peter took into his head to kiss the maiden's rosy lips with all his heart, without first looking well about him; and that same Evil One — may the son of a dog dream of the holy cross! — caused the old grey-beard, like a fool, to open the cottage door at that same moment. Korzh was petrified, dropped his jaw, and clutched at the door for support. Those unlucky kisses completely stunned him.

Recovering himself, he took his grandfather's hunting whip from the wall, and was about to belabour Peter's back with it, when Pidorka's little six-year-old brother Ivas rushed up from somewhere or other, and, grasping his father's legs with his little hands, screamed out, "Daddy, daddy! don't beat Peter!" What was to be done? A father's heart is not made of stone. Hanging the whip again on the wall, he led Peter quietly from the house. "If you ever show yourself in my cottage again, or even under the windows, look out, Peter, for, by heaven, your black moustache will disappear; and your black locks, though wound twice about your ears, will take leave of your pate, or my name is not Terentiy Korzh." So saying, he gave him such a taste of his fist in the nape of his neck, that all grew dark before Peter, and he flew headlong out of the place.

So there was an end of their kissing. Sorrow fell upon our turtle doves; and a rumour grew rife in the village that a certain Pole, all embroidered with gold, with moustaches, sabre, spurs, and pockets jingling like the bells of the bag with which our sacristan Taras goes through the church every day, had begun to frequent Korzh's house. Now, it is well known why a father has visitors when there is a black-browed daughter about. So, one day, Pidorka burst into tears, and caught the hand of her brother Ivas. "Ivas, my dear! Ivas, my love! fly to Peter, my child of gold, like an arrow from a bow. Tell him all: I would have loved his brown eyes, I would have kissed his fair face, but my fate decrees otherwise. More than one handkerchief have I wet with burning tears. I am sad and heavy at heart. And my own father is my enemy. I will not marry the Pole, whom I do not love. Tell him they are making ready for a wedding, but there will be no music at our wedding: priests will sing instead of pipes and viols. I shall not dance with my bridegroom: they will carry me out. Dark, dark will be my dwelling of maple wood; and, instead of chimneys, a cross will stand upon the roof."

Peter stood petrified, without moving from the spot, when the innocent child lisped out Pidorka's words to him. "And I, wretched man, had thought to go to the Crimea and Turkey, to win gold and return to thee, my beauty! But it may not be. We have been overlooked by the evil eye. I too shall have a wedding, dear one; but no ecclesiastics will be present at that wedding. The black crow instead of the pope will caw over me; the bare plain will be my dwelling; the dark blue cloud my roof-tree. The eagle will claw out my brown eyes: the rain will wash my Cossack bones, and the whirlwinds dry them. But what am I? Of what should I complain? 'Tis clear God willed it so. If I am to be lost, then so be it!" and he went straight to the tavern.

My late grandfather's aunt was somewhat surprised at seeing Peter at the tavern, at an hour when good men go to morning mass; and stared at him as though in a dream when he called for a jug of brandy, about half a pailful. But the poor fellow tried in vain to drown his woe. The vodka stung his tongue like nettles, and tasted more bitter than wormwood. He flung the jug from him upon the ground.

"You have sorrowed enough, Cossack," growled a bass voice behind him. He looked round — it was Basavriuk! Ugh, what a face! His hair was like a brush, his eyes like those of a bull. "I know what you lack: here it is." As he spoke he jingled a leather purse which hung from his girdle and smiled diabolically. Peter shuddered. "Ha, ha, ha! how it shines!" he roared, shaking out ducats into his hands: "ha, ha, ha! how it jingles! And I only ask one thing for a whole pile of such shiners."

"It is the Evil One!" exclaimed Peter. "Give me them! I'm ready for anything!"

They struck hands upon it, and Basavriuk said, "You are just in time, Peter: to-morrow is St. John the Baptist's day. Only on this one night in the year does the fern blossom. I will await you at midnight in the Bear's ravine."

I do not believe that chickens await the hour when the housewife brings their corn with as much anxiety as Peter awaited the evening. He kept looking to see whether the shadows of the trees were not lengthening, whether the sun was not turning red towards setting; and, the longer he watched, the more impatient he grew. How long it was! Evidently, God's day had lost its end somewhere. But now the sun has set. The sky is red only on one side, and it is already growing dark. It grows colder in the fields. It gets gloomier and gloomier, and at last quite dark. At last! With heart almost bursting from his bosom, he set out and cautiously made his way down through the thick woods into the deep hollow called the Bear's ravine. Basavriuk was already waiting there. It was so dark that you could not see a yard before you. Hand in hand they entered the ravine, pushing through the luxuriant thorn-bushes and stumbling at almost every step. At last they reached an open spot. Peter looked about him: he had never chanced to come there before. Here Basavriuk halted.

"Do you see before you three hillocks? There are a great many kinds of flowers upon them. May some power keep you from plucking even one of them. But as soon as the fern blossoms, seize it, and look not round, no matter what may seem to be going on behind thee."

Peter wanted to ask some questions, but behold Basavriuk was no longer there. He approached the three hillocks — where were the flowers? He saw none. The wild steppe-grass grew all around, and hid everything in its luxuriance. But the lightning flashed; and before him was a whole bed of flowers, all wonderful, all strange: whilst amongst them there were also the simple fronds of fern. Peter doubted his senses, and stood thoughtfully before them, arms akimbo.

"What manner of prodigy is this? why, one can see these weeds ten times a day. What is there marvellous about them? Devil's face must be mocking me!"

But behold! the tiny flower-bud of the fern reddened and moved as though alive. It was a marvel in truth. It grew larger and larger, and glowed like a burning coal. The tiny stars of light flashed up, something burst softly, and the flower opened before his eyes like a flame, lighting the others about it.

"Now is the time," thought Peter, and extended his hand. He saw hundreds of hairy hands reach also for the flower from behind him, and there was a sound of scampering in his rear. He half closed his eyes, and plucked sharply at the stalk, and the flower remained in his hand.

All became still.

Upon a stump sat Basavriuk, quite blue like a corpse. He did not move so much as a finger. Hi eyes were immovably fixed on something visible to him alone; his mouth was half open and speechless. Nothing stirred around. Ugh! it was horrible! But then a whistle was heard which made Peter's heart grow cold within him; and it seemed to him that the grass whispered, and the flowers began to talk among themselves in delicate voices, like little silver bells, while the trees rustled in murmuring contention; — Basavriuk's face suddenly became full of life, and his eyes sparkled. "The witch has just returned," he muttered between his teeth. "Hearken, Peter: a charmer will stand before you in a moment; do whatever she commands; if not — you are lost forever."

Then he parted the thorn-bushes with a knotty stick and before him stood a tiny farmhouse. Basavriuk smote it with his fist, and the wall trembled. A large black dog ran out to meet them, and with a whine transformed itself into a cat and flew straight at his eyes.

"Don't be angry, don't be angry, you old Satan!" said Basavriuk, employing such words as would have made a good man stop his ears. Behold, instead of a cat, an old woman all bent into a bow, with a face wrinkled like a baked apple, and a nose and chin like a pair of nutcrackers.

"A fine charmer!" thought Peter; and cold chills ran down his back. The witch tore the flower from his hand, stooped and muttered over it for a long time, sprinkling it with some kind of water. Sparks flew from her mouth, and foam appeared on her lips.

"Throw it away," she said, giving it back to Peter.

Peter threw it, but what wonder was this? The flower did not fall straight to the earth, but for a long while twinkled like a fiery ball through the darkness, and swam through the air like a boat. At last it began to sink lower and lower, and fell so far away that the little star, hardly larger than a poppy-seed, was barely visible. "There!" croaked the old woman, in a dull voice: and Basavriuk, giving him a spade, said, "Dig here, Peter: you will find more gold than you or Korzh ever dreamed of."

Peter spat on his hands, seized the spade, pressed his foot on it, and turned up the earth, a second, a third, a fourth time. The spade clinked against something hard, and would go no further. Then his eyes began to distinguish a small, iron-bound coffer. He tried to seize it; but the chest began to sink into the earth, deeper, farther, and deeper still: whilst behind him he heard a laugh like a serpent's hiss.

"No, you shall not have the gold until you shed human blood," said the witch, and she led up to him a child of six, covered with a white sheet, and indicated by a sign that he was to cut off his head.

Peter was stunned. A trifle, indeed, to cut off a man's, or even an innocent child's, head for no reason whatever! In wrath he tore off the sheet enveloping the victim's head, and behold! before him stood Ivas. The poor child crossed his little hands, and hung his head. Peter flew at the witch with the knife like a madman, and was on the point of laying hands on her.

"What did you promise for the girl?" thundered Basavriuk; and like a shot he was on his back. The witch stamped her foot: a blue flame flashed from the earth and illumined all within it. The earth became transparent as if moulded of crystal; and all that was within it became visible, as if in the palm of the hand. Ducats, precious stones in chests and pots, were piled in heaps beneath the very spot they stood on. Peter's eyes flashed, his mind grew troubled. . . . He grasped the knife like a madman, and the innocent blood spurted into his eyes. Diabolical laughter resounded on all sides. Misshapen monsters flew past him in flocks. The witch, fastening her hands in the headless trunk, like a wolf, drank its blood. His head whirled. Collecting all his strength, he set out to run. Everything grew red before him. The trees seemed steeped in blood, and burned and groaned. The sky glowed and threatened. Burning points, like lightning, flickered before his eyes. Utterly exhausted, he rushed into his miserable hovel and fell to the ground like a log. A death-like sleep overpowered him.

Two days and two nights did Peter sleep, without once awakening. When he came to himself, on the third day, he looked long at all the corners of his hut, but in vain did he endeavour to recollect what had taken place; his memory was like a miser's pocket, from which you cannot entice a quarter of a kopek. Stretching himself, he heard something clash at his feet. He looked, there were two bags of gold. Then only, as if in a dream, he recollected that he had been seeking for treasure, and that something had frightened him in the woods.

Korzh saw the sacks — and was mollified. "A fine fellow, Peter, quite unequalled! yes, and did I not love him? Was he not to me as my own son?" And the old fellow repeated this fiction until he wept over it himself. Pidorka began to tell Peter how some passing gipsies had stolen Ivas; but he could not even recall him — to such a degree had the Devil's influence darkened his mind! There was no reason for delay. The Pole was dismissed, and the wedding-feast prepared; rolls were baked, towels and handkerchiefs embroidered; the young people were seated at table; the wedding-loaf was cut; guitars, cymbals, pipes, viols sounded, and pleasure was rife.

A wedding in the olden times was not like one of the present day. My grandfather's aunt used to tell how the maidens — in festive head-dresses of yellow, blue, and pink ribbons, above which they bound gold braid; in thin chemisettes embroidered on all the seams with red silk, and strewn with tiny silver flowers; in morocco shoes, with high iron heels — danced the gorlitza as swimmingly as peacocks, and as wildly as the whirlwind; how the youths — with their ship-shaped caps upon their heads, the crowns of gold brocade, and two horns projecting, one in front and another behind, of the very finest black lambskin; in tunics of the finest blue silk with red borders — stepped forward one by one, their arms akimbo in stately form, and executed the gopak; how the lads — in tall Cossack caps, and light cloth gaberdines, girt with silver embroidered belts, their short pipes in their teeth — skipped before them and talked nonsense. Even Korzh as he gazed at the young people could not help getting gay in his old age. Guitar in hand, alternately puffing at his pipe and singing, a brandy-glass upon his head, the greybeard began the national dance amid loud shouts from the merry-makers.

What will not people devise in merry mood? They even began to disguise their faces till they did not look like human beings. On such occasions one would dress himself as a Jew, another as the Devil: they would begin by kissing each other, and end by seizing each other by the hair. God be with them! you laughed till you held your sides. They dressed themselves in Turkish and Tatar garments. All upon them glowed like a conflagration, and then they began to joke and play pranks .
. . .

An amusing thing happened to my grandfather's aunt, who was at this wedding. She was wearing an ample Tatar robe, and, wine-glass in hand, was entertaining the company.

The Evil One instigated one man to pour vodka over her from behind. Another, at the same moment, evidently not by accident, struck a light, and held it to her. The flame flashed up, and poor aunt, in terror, flung her dress off, before them all. Screams, laughter, jests, arose as if at a fair. In a word, the old folks could not recall so merry a wedding.

Pidorka and Peter began to live like a gentleman and lady. There was plenty of everything and everything was fine . . . . But honest folk shook their heads when they marked their way of living. "From the Devil no good can come," they unanimously agreed. "Whence, except from the tempter of orthodox people, came this wealth? Where else could he have got such a lot of gold from? Why, on the very day that he got rich, did Basavriuk vanish as if into thin air?"

Say, if you can, that people only imagine things! A month had not passed, and no one would have recognised Peter. He sat in one spot, saying no word to any one; but continually thinking and seemingly trying to recall something. When Pidorka succeeded in getting him to speak, he appeared to forget himself, and would carry on a conversation, and even grow cheerful; but if he inadvertently glanced at the sacks, "Stop, stop! I have forgotten," he would cry, and again plunge into reverie and strive to recall something. Sometimes when he sat still a long time in one place, it seemed to him as though it were coming, just coming back to mind, but again all would fade away. It seemed as if he was sitting in the tavern: they brought him vodka; vodka stung him; vodka was repulsive to him. Some one came along and struck him on the shoulder; but beyond that everything was veiled in darkness before him. The perspiration would stream down his face, and he would sit exhausted in the same place.

What did not Pirdorka do? She consulted the sorceresses; and they poured out fear, and brewed stomach ache[2] — but all to no avail. And so the summer passed. Many a Cossack had mowed and reaped; many a Cossack, more enterprising than the rest, had set off upon an expedition. Flocks of ducks were already crowding the marshes, but there was not even a hint of improvement.

It was red upon the steppes. Ricks of grain, like Cossack's caps, dotted the fields here and there. On the highway were to be encountered waggons loaded with brushwood and logs. The ground had become more solid, and in places was touched with frost. Already had the snow begun to fall and the branches of the trees were covered with rime like rabbit-skin. Already on frosty days the robin redbreast hopped about on the snow-heaps like a foppish Polish nobleman, and picked out grains of corn; and children, with huge sticks, played hockey upon the ice; while their fathers lay quietly on the stove, issuing forth at intervals with lighted pipes in their lips, to growl, in regular fashion, at the orthodox frost, or to take the air, and thresh the grain spread out in the barn. At last the snow began to melt, and the ice slipped away: but Peter remained the same; and, the more time went on, the more morose he grew. He sat in the cottage as though nailed to the spot, with the sacks of gold at his feet. He grew averse

---

2   "To pour out fear" refers to a practice resorted to in case of fear. When it is desired to know what caused this, melted lead or wax is poured into water, and the object whose form it assumes is the one which frightened the sick person; after this, the fear departs. Sonyashnitza is brewed for giddiness and pain in the bowels. To this end, a bit of stump is burned, thrown into a jug, and turned upside down into a bowl filled with water, which is placed on the patient's stomach: after an incantation, he is given a spoonful of this water to drink.

to companionship, his hair grew long, he became terrible to look at; and still he thought of but one thing, still he tried to recall something, and got angry and ill-tempered because he could not. Often, rising wildly from his seat, he gesticulated violently and fixed his eyes on something as though desirous of catching it: his lips moving as though desirous of uttering some long-forgotten word, but remaining speechless. Fury would take possession of him: he would gnaw and bite his hands like a man half crazy, and in his vexation would tear out his hair by the handful, until, calming down, he would relapse into forgetfulness, as it were, and then would again strive to recall the past and be again seized with fury and fresh tortures. What visitation of God was this?

Pidorka was neither dead not alive. At first it was horrible for her to remain alone with him in the cottage; but, in course of time, the poor woman grew accustomed to her sorrow. But it was impossible to recognise the Pidorka of former days. No blushes, no smiles: she was thin and worn with grief, and had wept her bright eyes away. Once some one who took pity on her advised her to go to the witch who dwelt in the Bear's ravine, and enjoyed the reputation of being able to cure every disease in the world. She determined to try that last remedy: and finally persuaded the old woman to come to her. This was on St. John's Eve, as it chanced. Peter lay insensible on the bench, and did not observe the newcomer. Slowly he rose, and looked about him. Suddenly he trembled in every limb, as though he were on the scaffold: his hair rose upon his head, and he laughed a laugh that filled Pidorka's heart with fear.

"I have remembered, remembered!" he cried, in terrible joy; and, swinging a hatchet round his head, he struck at the old woman with all his might. The hatchet penetrated the oaken door nearly four inches. The old woman disappeared; and a child of seven, covered in a white sheet, stood in the middle of the cottage. . . . The sheet flew off. "Ivas!" cried

Pidorka, and ran to him; but the apparition became covered from head to foot with blood, and illumined the whole room with red light . . . .

She ran into the passage in her terror, but, on recovering herself a little, wished to help Peter. In vain! the door had slammed to behind her, so that she could not open it. People ran up, and began to knock: they broke in the door, as though there were but one mind among them. The whole cottage was full of smoke; and just in the middle, where Peter had stood, was a heap of ashes whence smoke was still rising. They flung themselves upon the sacks: only broken potsherds lay there instead of ducats. The Cossacks stood with staring eyes and open mouths, as if rooted to the earth, not daring to move a hair, such terror did this wonder inspire in them.

I do not remember what happened next. Pidorka made a vow to go upon a pilgrimage, collected the property left her by her father, and in a few days it was as if she had never been in the village. Whither she had gone, no one could tell. Officious old women would have despatched her to the same place whither Peter had gone; but a Cossack from Kief reported that he had seen, in a cloister, a nun withered to a mere skeleton who prayed unceasingly. Her fellow-villagers recognised her as Pidorka by the tokens — that no one heard her utter a word; and that she had come on foot, and had brought a frame for the picture of God's mother, set with such brilliant stones that all were dazzled at the sight.

But this was not the end, if you please. On the same day that the Evil One made away with Peter, Basavriuk appeared again; but all fled from him. They knew what sort of a being he was — none else than Satan, who had assumed human form in order to unearth treasures; and, since treasures do not yield to unclean hands, he seduced the young. That same year, all deserted their earthen huts and collected in a village;

but even there there was no peace on account of that accursed Basavriuk.

My late grandfather's aunt said that he was particularly angry with her because she had abandoned her former tavern, and tried with all his might to revenge himself upon her. Once the village elders were assembled in the tavern, and, as the saying goes, were arranging the precedence at the table, in the middle of which was placed a small roasted lamb, shame to say. They chattered about this, that, and the other — among the rest about various marvels and strange things. Well, they saw something; it would have been nothing if only one had seen it, but all saw it, and it was this: the sheep raised his head, his goggling eyes became alive and sparkled; and the black, bristling moustache, which appeared for one instant, made a significant gesture at those present. All at once recognised Basavriuk's countenance in the sheep's head; my grandfather's aunt thought it was on the point of asking for vodka. The worthy elders seized their hats and hastened home.

Another time, the church elder himself, who was fond of an occasional private interview with my grandfather's brandy-glass, had not succeeded in getting to the bottom twice, when he beheld the glass bowing very low to him. "Satan take you, let us make the sign of the cross over you!"— And the same marvel happened to his better half. She had just begun to mix the dough in a huge kneading-trough when suddenly the trough sprang up. "Stop, stop! where are you going?" Putting its arms akimbo, with dignity, it went skipping all about the cottage — you may laugh, but it was no laughing matter to our grandfathers. And in vain did Father Athanasii go through all the village with holy water, and chase the Devil through all the streets with his brush. My late grandfather's aunt long complained that, as soon as it was dark, some one came knocking at her door and scratching at the wall.

Well! All appears to be quiet now in the place where our village stands; but it was not so very long ago — my father was still alive — that I remember how a good man could not pass the ruined tavern which a dishonest race had long managed for their own interest. From the smoke-blackened chimneys smoke poured out in a pillar, and rising high in the air, rolled off like a cap, scattering burning coals over the steppe; and Satan (the son of a dog should not be mentioned) sobbed so pitifully in his lair that the startled ravens rose in flocks from the neighbouring oak-wood and flew through the air with wild cries.